Contents

A Note About This Story

The title of this book comes from the story of the first man and woman on Earth – Adam and Eve. Adam and Eve lived in the Garden of Eden beside a beautiful river. They were happy together until something came and changed their lives.

The Island of Unimak

The Aleutian Islands are off the south coast of Alaska. They are in the Bering Sea which is part of the Pacific Ocean. There are many islands, but very few people live on them. The people who live on the Aleutian Islands hunt and fish. They sell the fish and the skins of animals that they catch.

One of the Aleutian Islands is called Unimak. There are lots of birds and wild animals on this island. The Arctic fox and the dangerous Kodiak bear live on Unimak. It is one of the loneliest places in the world.

There is a volcano on Unimak. It is over 3,000 metres high. In winter, the volcano is covered with snow. In spring, the snow melts and the water flows into a little river. This river runs into the sea in the west.

For a long time no one lived on Unimak. Then, during the Second World War, some American soldiers went there. They built a concrete radar post. But after the war, the soldiers left and grass grew over the empty radar post. People forgot about it.

BERING SEA

DUTCH HARBOUR

UNIMAK ISLAND

PACIFIC OCEAN

UNALASKA ISLAND

RUSSIA   ALASKA (U.S)

ALEUTIAN ISLANDS

radar post

Arctic fox

rabbit

Kodiak bear

Northern fur seal

seaweed (kelp)

salmon trap

salmon

5

The People in This Story

Jim Lee

Tania

Jess

Eric

Howard
Hamilton
Crawford

1

Jim and Tania

Jim Lee was an American. He was forty-seven years old and tall with grey hair. Jim was a good hunter and sailor but he was ugly. He had been wounded while he was fighting in the Second World War. There was a long, deep scar on the left side of his face.

Jim lived in Dutch Harbour, a fishing port 250 kilometres from Unimak. Most fishermen from Dutch Harbour never took their boats near Unimak. The grey sea round the island was dangerous and full of rocks. Only Jim Lee went to Unimak. He often hunted there and he knew about the radar post. Jim sometimes slept in the radar post when the weather was bad.

One day, Jim met an Aleut girl in Dutch Harbour. She worked in a bar for sailors and hunters. Jim took her to the Church of Saint Peter and married her there.

Jim's wife's name was Tania. She was eighteen years old and pretty. Tania was an Aleut. Her skin was dark and her eyes were small and narrow. Jim's friends were surprised when he married her.

'She's an Aleut!' they said. 'Why have you married her? White men don't marry Aleuts.'

A few days later, people in Dutch Harbour were even more surprised. Jim and Tania left Dutch Harbour in Jim's boat. Jim was taking his wife with him to Unimak. They were going to live there.

'Jim and the Aleut woman won't stay there very long,' they said. 'She'll probably leave him on Unimak. It's too lonely there. She'll come back without him!'

But the people of Dutch Harbour were wrong. Jim and Tania went to Unimak and lived happily there.

2

The Golden Seal

When Jim and Tania arrived on Unimak, they went to the old radar post.

'We'll make our home here,' said Jim.

They built a hut on top of the old radar post. This was their new home. They built another hut for storing the pelts – the skins of the dead animals. And there was a hut for smoking the fish.

Everything on Unimak belonged to Jim and Tania – fish, birds and animals. In winter, they trapped Arctic foxes. In summer, they shot rabbits and Kodiak bears. They made traps for salmon, too. Jim and Tania put their traps in the river and caught lots of salmon. Then they smoked the salmon over a fire in the hut.

But Jim was not completely happy. He had come to Unimak for a special reason; he hoped to catch a golden seal.

Golden seals are very beautiful, but there are very few of them in the Aleutian Islands. The seals spend most of their lives at sea. They come to land only when there is a storm. They escape from the storm by climbing onto rocks on an island. Then they are sometimes shot by hunters. But this does not happen often.

Jim had been in the Aleutian Islands for over forty years. In that time only twelve golden seals had been shot. And seven of these had been shot near Unimak.

The pelt of a golden seal is very valuable. In Dutch Harbour, people had paid 2,000 dollars for a pelt. Jim wanted to shoot a golden seal because he wanted 2,000 dollars. But there was another reason – a much more important reason. Jim wanted to show everybody in Dutch Harbour that he was the most skilful hunter in the Aleutian Islands. That was why he decided to live on Unimak.

Jim and Tania lived on the southern shore of Unimak. Their home was on a long line of rocks and sandhills. Jim spent a lot of time looking at the rocks and the sea. One day he hoped to see a golden seal.

But eight years passed and Jim did not see any golden seals.

In those eight years, Jim and Tania had two children. Eric, their son, was seven and Jess, their daughter, was three. They lived happily together on Unimak.

In eight years, Jim and Tania went back to Dutch Harbour three times. They bought stores and sold their pelts. Then they sailed back to Unimak.

Jim never enjoyed these visits to Dutch Harbour. Some of the men there laughed at him because he was ugly. And they laughed at him because he had married an Aleut woman.

'One day,' Jim thought, 'I'll show them the pelt of a golden seal and I'll laugh at them.'

But Tania did not want Jim to find a golden seal. She was afraid of having so much money. She was happy on Unimak. She did not want her life to change.

3

Waiting for the Storm

In the Aleutians, the summer of 1960 was warm and dry. On Unimak it was very hot. There was only a little snow on top of the volcano and only a little water in the river. Many of the flowers died.

Jim Lee knew that there was going to be a storm soon. The weather was much too hot. Summer storms in the Aleutians are very dangerous because they happen very suddenly.

Early one morning, Jim climbed one of the sandhills. He reached the top and looked around him. The sun was just rising. Below him, the island looked beautiful in the dawn light. Nothing moved. The sea was very calm and there was no wind at all.

There were small groups of sea-birds sitting on the sand. They were not moving and made no noise.

Then, Jim saw something unusual. He walked down to the edge of the sea. The water was covered with seaweed. Jim was worried. He knew why the seaweed had come to Unimak. Far away the storm had torn the seaweed from the bottom of the sea. Jim Lee knew the storm was coming to Unimak.

Jim looked at the sky. It was blue and clear. He looked at the sea. It was calm. But Jim knew that the storm was not far away now. He walked back to the hut.

The children were playing outside.

'Eric! Jess!' he shouted. 'Come and help me. We must cover the windows with wood.'

11

Tania helped Jim to pull the boat onto the land. They tied it down with ropes. Then they brought the food and water inside the hut.

'Stay close to the hut,' Jim told the children.

Then they waited for the storm to break.

4

The Storm Breaks

They waited all day, but the storm did not break.

That night it was very hot. There was no wind. Jim and his family did not sleep. The children were worried and Tania was frightened. Aleuts believe that storms happen because the gods are angry. All night, Tania sat by the door of the hut.

Next morning the sea was covered with seaweed. It was everywhere. Jim had never seen the sea like this before. Tania held his hand. They were both worried.

After breakfast, Jim said, 'Let's all go and pull in the salmon traps. We lost three of our traps in the last storm.'

But Eric did not want to go. The little boy had taken his father's binoculars and was looking at the seaweed. When his parents came out of the hut, he jumped up.

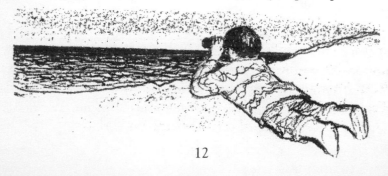

'Can I have your binoculars, Dad?' asked Eric.

'You've already got them!' replied his father.

'But can I keep them?' asked Eric.

'Yes, you can,' said Jim. 'But first you must come and help us with the salmon traps in the river. When we've finished, we'll both go to the top of the sandhills. We can watch the seaweed from there.'

Jim and Tania walked with Jess and Eric towards the river.

'Dad, golden seals live in seaweed, don't they?' Eric asked.

'Yes,' said Jim. 'They do.'

Now they knew what Eric wanted to look for!

Jim and Tania went into the river and took out the traps. Eric helped them for a short time.

'Dad! Can I go home now?' he asked.

'What's wrong?' asked Jim.

'I've got a headache,' replied Eric.

'All right,' said Jim. 'But go straight home.'

'Thanks, Dad,' said Eric.

'Now listen, Eric,' said Jim. 'There's going to be a storm soon. Promise you'll go straight home.'

'I promise!' said Eric, and walked off.

'He'll be back home in less than ten minutes,' Jim told himself. Jim had taught the children never to break a promise.

It was easy to pull in the salmon traps. They were all empty. The salmon had hidden in the mud. The sea-birds knew the storm was coming. They had disappeared too. Even though they were standing in the water Jim and Tania felt hot. There was no wind at all.

Jim looked at the sky. It was hard and bright.

'I think it's time we went back now,' Jim said.

They pulled all the traps out of the river. Then they picked up little Jess and walked towards the hut.

'Jim! Something's going to happen!' said Tania.

'Only a storm,' replied Jim.

'No, Jim, something else is going to happen. I know!'

Jim held Tania's hand.

Suddenly they felt the wind around their feet. Dead leaves flew in the air. Jim put Jess on his shoulders and they walked more quickly.

Several minutes later, they looked at the seaweed. It was moving up and down. There were big waves under it. Then the seaweed opened and big waves ran on to the shore. Jim put his daughter under his arm and began to run.

'Quick. Run!' he shouted to Tania.

'Eric!' shouted Tania, when they reached the hut. 'Eric! Eric!' There was no reply.

Inside the hut, Jim lit a lantern. His hands were shaking.

5

In the Storm Hut

But Eric was safe. He was sheltering from the storm not far from home.

When he left his parents, he crossed the river and climbed a sandhill. He looked through his father's binoculars. First he saw his home in the distance. He was not too far away. He had kept his promise.

Then he looked out to sea. The seaweed was moving. Eric lay down on the sandhill and watched the seaweed through the binoculars. Soon he had forgotten everything – golden seals, his family, the storm.

But suddenly the seaweed broke open. Waves hit the shore. Eric knew something was wrong. He jumped up. A huge cloud covered the sky and the wind was blowing.

Eric was afraid, but he did not run towards home. Home was too far away.

'Storms are dangerous,' his father had always told him. 'Find somewhere to shelter at once. Never stay out in the open.'

Jim had built several storm huts near the sea. These small huts were to shelter in when the weather was very bad. There was a hut not far away. Eric ran towards it. He was running for his life.

The storm broke. The sky grew darker and the wind stronger. A hundred metres from the hut, the wind knocked Eric down. The little boy did not get up. He crawled towards the storm hut on his hands and knees.

At last he reached the hut and crawled inside. There was no chimney and no windows. Eric immediately noticed a strange smell. It came from the other side of the hut. Then something moved.

The little boy stood up and looked into the darkness. Two eyes looked back at him. Something was in the hut. Was it a Kodiak bear? Eric was terrified. He wanted to run away, but then he remembered the storm outside.

Eric stood still and waited. But the animal did not attack him. It was large, but it was not a bear. What was it?

Eric found a metal box that Jim had left in the hut. He

opened it and took out a candle. Then he lit the candle and looked at the animal again.

Eric had never seen anything so beautiful. There, in front of him, was a golden seal! And beside the golden seal were her two pups.

'Oh!' he whispered. 'You're so beautiful. And so are your pups.'

One of the pups was frightened by Eric's voice. It fell away from its mother onto the ground. The golden seal looked at Eric.

'It's all right,' said the little boy. 'Don't worry. I'll pick up your baby for you.'

The golden seal watched Eric very carefully, but she did not attack him. Eric picked up the little pup and gave it back to her. Then he said, 'Are you hungry? Let's find something to eat.'

He looked in the metal box and found some chocolate and some smoked salmon.

'The chocolate's for me,' he told the golden seal. 'The salmon's for you.'

Eric pushed the food towards the golden seal, but she did not touch it. She watched him very carefully. Then Eric put the candle on the metal box and went to the door. Outside, the storm was blowing fiercely. Inside the hut, it was quiet and comfortable.

The golden seal lay on one side of the hut. Eric lay down on the other. He was eating chocolate – lots and lots of chocolate. And every time he took some chocolate, he pushed some salmon towards the golden seal.

At first, she did not look at it. Then, she tasted the nearest piece. She liked it, so Eric gave her some more. Soon he was putting the fish into her mouth.

There, in front of him, was a golden seal!

Outside, it was snowing. Inside the hut, Eric was cold. He found two blankets. He put one over the golden seal and the other one over himself. The hours passed slowly. Each hour was slower and colder than the one before. Then the candle went out and the little boy slept.

He woke up in the middle of the night. He was cold and began to cry. The golden seal looked at him from the other side of the hut. Her eyes were warm and red.

Eric stopped crying. He moved across the hut and lay down beside the golden seal. She was warm and soft. Very soon, Eric fell asleep.

6

Crawford the Hunter

A few hours before the storm broke, a ship was sailing close to the island of Unimak. The captain was Howard Hamilton Crawford and the crew were Aleuts.

Crawford was an evil man. He was a sailor and a hunter and everyone in Dutch Harbour disliked him.

And now, Howard Hamilton Crawford was hunting a golden seal. It was in the sea, not far away, swimming towards Unimak.

'Lower the small boat!' he shouted to the men. 'Give me a gun and some rope.'

The Aleuts brought Crawford a gun and some rope immediately.

'If the storm breaks, stay here,' said Crawford. 'Don't come and look for me. Bring the ship to Unimak after the storm. Wait for me there. OK?'

Then Crawford jumped into the small boat and started the outboard motor. He was hunting a golden seal at last!

An hour later, Crawford's boat was far away from the ship. The golden seal, in the distance, had nearly reached land. Crawford looked up at the sky. The storm was very near.

'I can't go back now,' he thought. 'I want the pelt of that golden seal.'

Crawford's boat was twenty metres from the shore when the storm broke. The boat turned over and Crawford was thrown into the sea. He had to swim for his life.

Very slowly, he came nearer to the shore. Then the wind and the waves caught him and threw him onto the sand. Crawford did not know it but he was not far from Jim Lee's home.

Crawford lay on the sand for some time. Then he stood up. There, in the distance, was a light.

'I must reach that light,' he thought. 'I must shelter from the storm.'

The wind blew Crawford over several times. Flying stones hit him. At last he crawled on his hands and knees towards the light.

7

Out in the Storm

The storm was very fierce. The wind was pushing at the walls and roof of the family hut. The lamp was swinging backwards and forwards. Suddenly the lamp smashed against a wall. Darkness! Silence! Then the door burst open and the wind blew a chair across the room.

Little Jess screamed and got out of her bed. Tania ran across the room and put her back in her bed. Jim threw himself at the door. He pushed with all his strength and shut it again. Behind him, Tania lit another lamp.

'Poor Eric,' said Tania. 'Poor boy!'

'He'll be all right,' said Jim. 'He'll go to one of the storm huts.'

But Jim was very worried about Eric. He listened to the angry noise of the storm outside. Was Eric sheltering in one of the storm huts? Perhaps. But perhaps Eric was out in the open. Jim decided he had to look for Eric. The storm was getting worse.

Jim tied a rope around his waist. He gave the other end to Tania.

'If I'm in trouble, I'll pull on the rope,' he said. 'Then you must pull me back into the hut.'

Sand blew into the hut when Jim opened the door.

'Jim! Don't go!' cried Tania. 'Oh, please don't go!'

But Jim had already crawled out on hands and knees into the storm. Tania was alone holding the other end of the rope.

Jim crawled out of the hut and into a terrible world. There was now no difference between the land, the sea and the sky. The storm was a mixture of sand, rain and wind. It was hard to breathe and the flying sand and stones cut his skin.

The wind hit Jim and knocked him flat. He tried to look around him. He did not see Eric. But was that a boat down there on the rocks? Was it really a boat? It was impossible to see.

Jim could not stay out in the storm any longer. He pulled on the rope. Slowly, Tania pulled him back to the hut. At last, he was at the door, then inside, and finally the door was shut.

'Oh, Jim! Oh, Jim!' said Tania, as she washed the blood from his face and hands. Then she tied bandages around his wounded hands.

'Don't worry,' said Jim. 'Eric's not outside. He's probably in one of the storm huts.'

They sat on the floor of the hut, drank cocoa, and listened to the noise of the storm. They did not talk because there was nothing to say. Eric was either alive in one of the storm huts. Or he was out in the storm, dead.

Suddenly Tania got up and stood very still. Her eyes were frightened.

'Jim. Don't ever change,' she said.

'Change?' asked Jim.

'Please,' said Tania, 'promise me you'll never change.'

Tania went and sat down beside Jim. 'I'm frightened, Jim,' she said. 'We've been too happy. The gods are angry. Now they're trying to destroy us.'

Then Tania jumped up, 'What's that?' she asked.

The wind was as strong as ever. But there was another noise, too. Something or someone was knocking at the door.

'Eric?' called Jim. 'Eric?'

'No!' screamed Tania. 'It's not Eric. It's the devil. Don't let him in!'

But then the door burst open. And a man was blown into the hut. His face and arms were covered in blood. Tania screamed as he fell at her feet.

But then the door burst open. And a man was blown into the hut.

Jim, Tania and Crawford

Tania looked at the man. She was terrified and ran to the corner of the hut. Jim pushed hard against the door and closed it. Then he started to pull the man across the floor.

'Help me lift him, Tania,' said Jim.

For a second she did not move. Then she picked up the man's feet and together they lifted him onto the bed.

Jim tried to open the man's anorak. But he could not because of the bandages on his hands.

'Can you open his anorak?' said Jim.

Now they saw the man's face. He was young and good-looking, but he was in pain.

'Poor man!' said Jim.

Tania had thought that he was the devil. Now she saw that he was a man and he was hurt. Blood was running down his face.

She brought some water, sat on the edge of the bed and washed his face. Then she tied a bandage around his head. The man's eyes half-opened and he looked at her and smiled.

'Jim!' said Tania. 'I think he's waking up.'

Jim walked over to the bed, but the man's eyes were closed again.

The storm continued. Jim and Tania could not sleep. They wanted to look for Eric as soon as the wind stopped blowing. They waited for hour after hour. Every now and then they looked at the man on the bed.

Tania thought that the man was watching them. But each time she went across and looked at him, his eyes were shut.

Then, a little after two o'clock, he sat up. He sat up slowly, holding his head. He looked round the hut. Then he saw Tania.

'Ah! I thought I was dreaming!' he said.

Tania jumped to her feet.

'I'll make you some cocoa,' she said.

'Thanks,' he replied.

He watched her go out of the room and then spoke to Jim.

'My name's Howard Crawford,' he said. 'Is that your woman, mister?'

'My wife,' said Jim.

'Ah,' replied the man. 'It's very kind of you to stay awake all night with me.'

'We're staying awake because of our son He's out there, in the storm. When the wind drops, we'll look for him,' said Jim.

'Poor kid,' said the man.

Crawford did not believe Jim and his wife. Crawford thought they were lying. He thought they had seen the golden seal.

'They want to go out and shoot my golden seal,' Crawford said to himself. 'I must watch them carefully.'

'Why were you out in the storm, mister?' asked Jim.

Crawford did not want to tell them.

'I was out in a small boat,' he said.

'But why were you in a small boat in the storm?' asked Jim.

'You're asking a lot of questions, mister,' said Crawford.

There was a long silence. Jim began to dislike the stranger.

Then Tania brought in the cocoa and gave it to Crawford. The man's face frightened her. She had seen men like him before, in Dutch Harbour.

Crawford drank the cocoa and began to feel stronger. He got off the bed and walked up and down.

'I'm all right now,' he said. 'I was lucky.'

Then he turned to Tania and said, 'You can have your bed now. I'll sleep on the floor.'

'You can stay on the bed,' said Tania. 'We're not using it tonight.'

The stranger looked at her thoughtfully.

'Oh, yes,' he said. 'You're staying awake because of your daughter.'

'Our son,' she said.

'Yes, I mean your son,' said Crawford. 'Will you start looking for him as soon as the wind drops?'

Tania nodded.

'I'll come with you,' said Crawford.

'No thanks, mister,' said Jim. 'You don't have to come

with us.'

Then Crawford lay down on the bed. He made himself comfortable and closed his eyes.

Jim and Tania knew that he was not sleeping. The man on the bed was watching them, hour after hour.

Later, the wind dropped and Jim and his family tried to leave the hut without the stranger. They wanted to go alone to look for Eric. But Crawford heard the door open.

'Wait for me!' he said.

'Are you sure you want to come?' asked Jim.

'Oh, yes!' said Crawford. 'I'm coming with you.'

Soon, the two men, Tania and Jess were walking in the snow. Jim turned round and looked back at the hut. As he turned he noticed something. The stranger was putting a revolver into his pocket.

9

The River

In the storm hut, Eric slept close to the golden seal. She kept him warm together with her pups.

Next morning, Eric woke up and went to the door and opened it. Snow blew into the hut. The storm was not so fierce now. He shut the door again.

'The storm's nearly over,' he told the golden seal. 'My father will come and look for me soon. He's a hunter. He shoots seals. But don't worry. I'll go home now and make him promise not to shoot you. You're my friend. He can't shoot you.'

Then Eric gave the last piece of smoked salmon to the seal. He put some chocolate in his pocket and left the hut.

Not far away, Jim, Tania, Jess and Crawford were walking along the shore. Jim and Tania were looking for Eric. Crawford was secretly looking for the golden seal.

Jim and Tania decided to turn away from the sea. Crawford stayed behind on the shore.

'Perhaps they really are looking for their son,' he thought.

Jim, Tania and Jess were walking by the river. The river was full of water and it was flowing fast. It was going to be very difficult to cross the river.

'Look!' said Jim. 'Look, Tania, look!'

His voice was quiet and he pointed to the far side of the river. There in the distance, was the little boy walking through the snow.

'Eric!' said Tania. 'Oh, thank God. It's Eric!'

She was so happy that she burst into tears. They stood on the river bank waving to Eric. Eric ran towards them on the other side of the river.

Then Crawford arrived.

'Is that your boy?' he asked.

Jim nodded.

'Good!' Crawford thought to himself. 'They really have come to look for the boy. They don't know anything about my golden seal. That makes things much easier for me. I'll look for the golden seal while they take the boy home.'

'How is the boy going to get across the river?' asked Crawford.

'I don't know,' said Jim. 'It'll be difficult.'

Jim put one of his bandaged hands into the water. The water was very cold and the river was running fast.

'I think this is the best place to cross,' said Jim. 'Or we will have to go ten kilometres up the river.'

Crawford wanted to look for the golden seal as soon as possible. He did not want to waste time.

'We can cross here,' said Crawford. 'How much rope have you got with you?'

'Eighty metres,' replied Jim.

'I'll swim across with it,' said Crawford.

'No, I'll go,' said Jim. 'Eric's my son.'

'But you can't swim with those bandages on your hands,' said Crawford.

'Thanks, mister,' said Jim. 'But I'll swim across and get him.'

He put down the rope and started to take the bandages off his hands.

'No, Jim,' said Tania. 'Look at your hands! You won't be able to hold the rope. Let me go across. Please!'

At the same time she looked at Crawford. Crawford understood what she wanted to say, 'You're a man. Why don't you go?' He smiled at her.

'Don't worry, Tania,' said Jim. 'I'll be all right.'

But it was too late. Crawford had already tied the rope around his waist and walked into the water.

10

Crossing the River

Jim was angry, but there was nothing he could do. Crawford threw the rope to Tania.

'Tie it around that rock,' said Crawford.

'I hope he knows what he's doing,' Jim said to Tania. He looked at her. She was watching Crawford with great interest.

Crawford was crossing the river slowly. The river was running quickly, and Crawford moved carefully between the rocks. Most of the time, he could walk. The water came up to his waist or to his shoulders. But sometimes he had to swim. There were moments of danger when his head disappeared below the water. But Crawford was a powerful swimmer.

Jim watched and felt better. Crawford was nearly at the other bank. Then Jim looked at Tania. She was watching Crawford excitedly. Suddenly Jim became jealous.

'Is Tania excited about seeing Eric again? Or is she in love with Crawford?' he asked himself.

Crawford crawled out of the water onto the opposite bank. He shook himself like a dog, and then spoke to Eric.

'Hello, kid. I'm Howard Crawford. I've come to help you across the river.'

'Why didn't my Dad come?' asked Eric.

'Your Dad hurt his hands in the storm,' replied Crawford.

Eric looked at Crawford. 'Did you get hurt in the storm, too?' he asked.

*Crawford crawled out of the water onto
the opposite bank.*

'Yes,' said Crawford. He took the bandage off his head and showed Eric a dark bruise on his skin.

'Did you get a bruise, too?' asked Crawford.

'Not a bruise,' said Eric. 'Something much, much, *much* better! Something I found. You can have three guesses.'

'Did you find a bag of gold?' asked Crawford.

'No,' said Eric, 'but you're nearly right.'

'Was it a bag of diamonds, then?' asked Crawford.

'No,' said Eric. 'That was a bad guess.'

Suddenly Crawford had an idea. 'Perhaps the boy has seen my golden seal,' he thought. 'No, that's impossible.'

Crawford looked up and saw Jim and Tania waving from the other river bank.

'Your Mum and Dad are waiting for us,' he said to Eric. 'It's time we went back.'

'But what about your third guess?' asked Eric. 'Try and guess what I found in the storm.'

'I'll think about it while we're crossing the river,' said Crawford. 'Climb on my back.'

Crawford took the rope and tied Eric onto his back. Then he walked back into the water.

The second crossing was more difficult than the first. Much more difficult. And Eric was very heavy. But soon the other bank was very near, and Jim was in the water beside Crawford. Still a few metres to go! Finally, Jim pulled Crawford onto the bank and untied Eric. Crawford lay down on the snow.

Tania and Jess were delighted to see Eric again. So was Jim. They talked excitedly for several minutes.

'I'm a fool,' thought Crawford. 'I crossed that river for a pretty girl's smile. Now her son is back and she leaves me lying in the snow!'

Then he felt an arm under his shoulders. It was Tania. She bandaged his head again and poured brandy into his mouth. Crawford looked up. Her lips were near his face. Her eyes were soft and gentle.

'I'm going to have a good time with this woman,' Crawford thought to himself.

'Thank you,' said Tania, 'for bringing my son back.'

Crawford held Tania's arm. His fingers tightened.

But suddenly there was fear in Tania's eyes. She jumped away from him and knocked over the bottle of brandy. Crawford was surprised.

'Jim,' Tania said. 'Let's go home!'

'Her husband's here,' Crawford thought to himself. 'Was he watching us?'

But Jim was talking to Eric. He had seen nothing.

11

The Secret

When they were walking back home, Eric pulled at his father's arm.

'What do you want, Eric?' asked Jim.

'I've got a secret, Dad,' said Eric. Then he looked round at the others. They were far away and could not hear.

'Dad,' he said, 'it's a secret between you and me. Promise me you won't tell anybody.'

Jim looked at his son. He remembered that Eric had broken a promise. Eric had promised to go straight home before the storm.

'Do you remember your promise?' said Jim. 'Didn't you break your promise to go home?'

'But I could see our hut all the time through the binoculars,' replied the little boy.

'Promises are very important, Eric,' said Jim. 'You promised to go straight home. But you didn't. You broke that promise.'

'I'm sorry, Dad,' said Eric. 'But now I want you to make a promise.'

'What do you want me to promise?' asked Jim.

'I've found something, Dad,' said Eric. 'Something very special. Promise you won't hurt her.'

'All right, Eric,' said Jim. He was thinking about Tania and Jess who were alone with Crawford.

'Dad, say "I promise",' said Eric.

'OK Eric, I promise,' said Jim.

Eric started talking very quickly, but Jim did not listen. He was still worried about Tania. Then, he suddenly understood what Eric was saying.

'. . . and her fur's soft and yellow like the sun. And she has two little babies. And she's a golden seal, Dad. And she's my friend.'

Jim sat down. He had waited for this moment for eight years. For eight years, he had searched for a golden seal. This was the chance he had always wanted!

'Kill the golden seal,' Jim thought to himself. 'If I kill the golden seal, I'll be rich! I'll be famous! People in Dutch Harbour will say I am the best hunter! I'll have everything I want!'

Jim was angry with himself. 'Why have I made this promise to Eric?' he thought 'At last there is a golden seal on Unimak!'

'Thanks for your promise, Dad,' said Eric. 'Now nobody will hurt her. I'm sure.'

And he took hold of his father's hand.

12

Jim Keeps His Promise

When they got back to the hut, they all had a hot meal. Then Crawford said, 'The weather's getting better. I think I'll go for a walk.'

Jim was surprised when Crawford walked down to the shore.

'What is he looking for?' asked Tania.

Jim did not reply. But he was sure that Crawford was looking for the golden seal. He pulled open a drawer. He took out a revolver and gave it to Tania.

'Listen, Tania,' said Jim. 'I want you to carry this gun, all the time. I want you to carry it while Crawford is on this island.'

'Oh, Jim!' said Tania. 'I don't need a gun!'

'Please, Tania,' said Jim. 'You never know what will happen!'

Tania took the gun from her husband and put it into the pocket of her skirt.

'Are you happier now, Jim?' she asked.

'Yes, much happier,' said Jim. 'And I'll tell you why. Eric and I are leaving you and Jess for a short time. We're going to the storm hut where he spent the night.'

Tania took hold of Jim's hand. 'Jim!' she said. 'What is happening?'

Jim looked at her. 'I can't tell her about the golden seal,' he thought. 'I can't tell her about my promise to Eric. And I can't tell her why Crawford is on Unimak.'

'I'm not sure what's happening,' said Jim. 'But I'll tell you when I *am* sure. I promise.'

Jim picked up his gun. A few minutes later, father and son were walking towards the storm hut.

'Come on, Dad! Run!' said Eric.

But Jim stopped. He raised his gun.

'Now listen, Eric,' said Jim. 'This golden seal is a friend of yours. But she doesn't know me. So we must be careful.'

Slowly, they walked to the storm hut. Then they looked inside. But the golden seal was not there.

'Did Crawford get here first?' Jim thought to himself. But he had not heard a shot from Crawford's gun. 'Perhaps Eric never saw a golden seal?' he thought. 'But no! There were golden hairs on the floor of the hut.'

'Your friend, the golden seal, left a short time ago,' said Jim. 'Perhaps we'll find her.'

They cleaned the storm hut and left some more salmon, candles and chocolate there. Then they went to look for the golden seal.

After an hour, Eric was very tired and very sad.

'She's not here, Dad,' he said. 'She's gone back to the sea.'

Jim looked at the sea. 'No,' he said. 'The waves are too big.'

'Perhaps she's in the pool at the top of that sandhill,' said Eric.

A few minutes later they were near the top of the hill.

'Be careful, Eric,' said Jim.

Then Eric stood still and pointed. 'There she is, Dad,' he said.

'Don't be frightened, golden seal,' said Eric. 'It's only me. I'm your friend.'

Jim pointed his gun at the seal. 'Eric! Don't go near her,' he said.

'It's all right, Dad. She knows me,' said Eric.

He threw a piece of salmon into the pool. For a minute, the golden seal did not move. Then she opened her mouth and the salmon was gone.

Eric was delighted. He walked to the edge of the pool. The golden seal swam towards him. Then she opened her mouth and Eric gave her some more salmon.

Jim's gun was ready to fire. 'Shoot her! Shoot her!' he thought. 'Two thousand dollars for her pelt! I'll be a famous hunter.'

Jim had waited for this moment for eight years. 'I can shoot the golden seal,' thought Jim. 'Then I can tell Eric it wanted to attack him.'

But no. He had made a promise to Eric. And Eric trusted him. 'No, I can't shoot her,' he thought. Jim put down his gun.

13
Danger!

The golden seal was Eric's friend. She was not dangerous. But danger was not far away.

A Kodiak bear sat watching father and son. The bear

Jim had waited for this moment for eight years.

was hungry and wanted to kill them.

The bear waited patiently. He was waiting for the moment to kill. His claws were long and sharp.

'It's time to go now, Eric,' said Jim. 'We'll keep the secret of the golden seal.'

'A secret?' asked Eric. 'Between you and me?'

'Yes. A secret between you and me and Mummy,' said Jim.

Eric was surprised. 'And not tell Mr Crawford?' he asked.

'No,' said Jim. 'We mustn't tell Howard Crawford.'

Then they turned towards home. Jim said nothing. He was thinking about Crawford and Tania.

But suddenly he saw a large shadow and long claws. A bear! Jim knew that bears were very dangerous. And he knew that his gun was not powerful enough to kill the bear.

Jim stopped Eric. 'Quiet!' he whispered.

Slowly and quietly they moved away in the opposite direction. They moved away from the bear. They walked down to the shore and hid behind some rocks.

Soon, the Kodiak bear thought that they had gone. He could not hear them because of the noise of the wind. And he could not smell them because the wind blew their scent away from him. The bear was angry and hungry. Twice he ran down to the sea. Once he came very near to Jim and Eric, but he did not find them.

The bear stopped and waited. Then he walked off towards the Lee family's home.

Jim and Eric were careful. They waited for ten minutes before they moved away from the rocks. Jim's gun was always ready to fire.

Once the bear came very near to Jim and Eric, but he did not find them.

Jim was thinking about the bear and not about Crawford and Tania. But suddenly they heard the noise of Tania's revolver.

Jim began to run home – faster and faster.

'Dad! Dad! Wait for me!' shouted Eric.

But Jim did not stop. He was worried about Tania. And where was Crawford?

14

Crawford and Tania

While Jim and Eric were with the golden seal, Crawford was searching on the shore. He was searching for the golden seal.

'The others don't know about my golden seal,' Crawford thought to himself! 'When I find her, I'll kill her.'

He walked and searched for hours, but he did not find her.

As he walked back to the hut, he thought about the Lee family. What a strange life, alone on this island!

'Perhaps this life is good for the scar-faced man,' thought Crawford. 'But it's terrible for the woman. How can she stay here with that ugly man? He's old enough to be her father!'

Crawford decided that Tania needed a change and some excitement in her life. 'I know she likes me,' he thought.

Soon he was near the hut. Tania was sitting outside. And she was alone.

Then Crawford remembered a story he had heard in Dutch Harbour. It was the story of an ugly man who married an Aleut barmaid. They had gone to live on a lonely island. Of course! Jim was the man! And Tania was the girl!

Tania looked up. 'Hello,' she said. 'Did you enjoy your walk?'

'Yes,' replied Crawford, and he sat down beside her.

'My husband will be back soon,' said Tania. 'I'm going to give Jess some food and get our dinner ready.'

'Forget your husband, Tania,' said Crawford.

'But I don't want to,' she replied. She was frightened.

Crawford followed her into the hut and pulled her towards him. He tried to kiss her. But, at that moment, she spat in his face. Crawford was very surprised.

'Keep back. Or I'll kill you!' said Tania. She pointed her revolver at Crawford's stomach.

Crawford laughed and took a step forward. And then another.

There was a loud noise as the gun fired. But Crawford felt no pain. He waited for the pain. It did not come! Tania had missed! Jess was in her bed, crying.

'You'll be sorry you shot at me,' said Crawford.

'Are you all right?' asked Tania.

Crawford nodded.

'We'll have to explain the noise of the gun,' said Tania.

'Explain it?' asked Crawford. 'Why?'

'My husband will know that I fired the gun,' replied Tania. 'He'll want to know why. And when he knows why, he'll kill you.'

'Oh no, Tania. You're wrong,' said Crawford. 'I'll kill your husband. I'm younger than he is. And stronger. And

41

'Keep back. Or I'll kill you!' said Tania.

I'm good with guns and knives.'

Tania was very frightened. She did not want the two men to fight.

'I'll tell my husband that I fired at a Kodiak bear,' she said.

'He won't believe you, Tania,' said Crawford.

'Yes,' she said. 'He'll believe me. I know he will.'

'Tell him what you like,' said Crawford. 'I don't care.'

Then Tania ran out of the hut with Jess and down to the shore. Jim and Eric were running towards them.

'Why did you shoot?' asked Jim.

'There was a Kodiak bear,' said Tania.

They believed her immediately. Tania was very surprised. Then she heard Eric say, 'Wasn't he a horrible bear, Mummy? He was chasing us, too!'

Tania sat down. She did not know whether to laugh or cry. Then Jim took her in his arms.

15

Jim's Problems

The Lee family and Crawford sat down to dinner. The two men were silent. Their dislike for each other was getting stronger. But nothing happened. They were too tired to argue. As soon as the meal was over, they all went to sleep.

Sleep brings dreams. And everyone on Unimak dreamt that night. The dreams of the adults were unhappy. Only the dreams of the children were happy. Eric dreamt that he was playing with the golden seal. They were playing in the beautiful river that ran out of Eden.

Jim woke up very early because he heard a noise. He listened. At the far end of the hut, a door closed quietly. Then he heard footsteps outside. Jim got up and went to look out of the window. Crawford was outside. He was walking down to the shore, carrying a gun.

Jim walked back to the bed. He looked at Tania. She was still asleep. Her face was pale and unhappy. Jim bent down and kissed her lips.

Tania spoke in her sleep. 'No,' she said. 'Please.'

Jim's fears suddenly came back. 'Perhaps it's true,' he thought. 'My wife is in love with Crawford.'

Jim went outside into the beautiful morning light. The storm had gone. But so many things had come with the storm … a golden seal, the promise to his son, Crawford. And now Tania was falling in love with Crawford.

'I must do something,' thought Jim. 'If I shoot the seal, then Crawford will leave. Everything will be all right again!'

The voice of the devil spoke to Jim. 'Break your promise. Shoot the golden seal. It's not for the money– the 2,000 dollars. You must shoot the seal to save your wife from Crawford. One shot between the golden seal's eyes – and everything will be all right.'

But Jim knew it was wrong to break a promise. It was wrong to break a promise to a child. His child.

'No,' said Jim. 'I will never break my promise to my son!'

Then Jim thought about Tania. 'I must talk to her about our problems,' he thought. And he walked back towards the hut.

16

Tania's Problems

When Jim got near the hut, he saw Tania. She had got up and was sitting outside, near the door. There were tears on her face.

Tania had woken up and found that Jim had gone. She had seen that Crawford had gone, too.

Then she had thought of the two men alone outside ... Crawford's knife in Jim's back. Jim's blood on the sand.

But it had only been a dream. Now she saw that Jim was safe.

'I shot at Crawford yesterday,' she thought to herself. 'But I wanted him. I have spent eight years on this island alone with Jim. It is a long time. In my bar in Dutch Harbour, there were lots of men.'

But then Tania remembered her wedding promise in the Church of Saint Peter. She had promised to love only Jim.

'No, I won't break my promise,' she thought. 'I mustn't! I can't!' And she felt much better.

Jim sat down beside Tania. Slowly, he told her about the golden seal and his promise to Eric.

Then Tania spoke to Jim about Crawford. She told Jim how she liked Crawford's smile.

'But now I've told you, I feel much better,' said Tania. 'I'm sorry, Jim, I'm sorry.'

'Tania,' said Jim, 'I'm going to put all our pelts onto the boat. I'm going to sail to Dutch Harbour. I'll take Crawford with me and leave him there.'

'But Jim,' said Tania, 'do you think Crawford will go

with you?'

Jim was very angry and picked up his gun. 'Tania,' he said, 'I'll make him go!'

Tania was afraid. 'No, Jim,' she said. 'Don't do that. That's what he's waiting for. Crawford's a bad man. He'll kill you. Then he will have everything he wants.'

Jim looked at her and understood. He was very angry. They had saved Crawford from the storm. And now Crawford was destroying their happiness.

'All right,' said Jim. 'I won't fight him. But I'll put everything on the boat. Perhaps he'll come with me to Dutch Harbour anyway.'

Jim and Tania spent the afternoon putting all the pelts into the boat. There were 168 skins from bears, foxes, rabbits and other animals.

It was September. And it was a bad month for selling pelts. But it was a valuable cargo.

At last the boat was ready. Jim, Tania and the children were in the hut when Crawford appeared again. He had searched the shore for nearly twelve hours. He had found nothing. He had not found the golden seal. Howard Hamilton Crawford was a very angry man!

17

Crawford Must Leave

Crawford had followed the golden seal to Unimak. Now he had searched the whole shore twice. And the waves around the island were still too strong. The seal could not leave.

Crawford was now certain that Jim had killed the golden seal.

'He's killed her and hidden her pelt,' thought Crawford. 'As soon as I leave, they'll take her pelt to Dutch Harbour.'

But Crawford had an idea.

'I'll stay here until I find the golden seal,' he thought. 'The ugly man and the girl won't like that!'

Inside the hut, Crawford kicked off his boots. Then he threw his gun on the floor.

Tania watched him silently.

'Dry this for me,' said Crawford and threw his coat to Tania. 'And my boots too.'

Tania stood still for a moment, then she bent down.

'Don't touch them, Tania,' said Jim. His hand was on

his gun. 'Leave us.'

'Be careful, Jim,' she whispered. 'Oh, please be careful.'
And Tania turned and walked out of the door.

'My wife isn't your servant, mister,' said Jim.

Crawford's gun was still on the floor. So he did not try
to fight Jim then.

'Why are you angry?' Crawford asked.

'I told you,' said Jim. 'Tania isn't your slave. The
storm's over now and you don't have to stay here any
longer. Tomorrow, I'm taking you back to Dutch Harbour.
My boat is ready. I'm sailing at seven o'clock tomorrow
morning. And you're coming with me!'

'And if I don't want to come?' asked Crawford.

Jim held up his gun. 'You'll come,' he said.

Then Jim picked up Crawford's gun from the floor. 'I'll keep this until we get to Dutch Harbour,' he said. Then he walked out.

Alone in the hut, Crawford was angry. 'Why didn't he kill me while he had the chance?' he thought. 'Next time, I'll kill him!'

18

A Guessing Game

Something exciting was happening. Eric was certain. His mother and father were whispering together. The boat was full of pelts. And everyone knew September was a bad month for selling pelts.

'It'll soon be bedtime,' thought Eric. 'I'll have to go inside and I won't know what has happened!'

'Eric!' said somebody.

It was not his father calling. It was not bedtime yet. Mr Crawford was calling him.

'Yes?' he said.

'Do you want to play a game?' asked Crawford.

'Oh, yes!' said Eric. 'What are we going to play?'

'I'll be a horse and you can ride on my back,' said Crawford.

Eric was not sure. That was a game his mother played with his little sister. But he said nothing and climbed onto Crawford's back.

The game was wonderful. Mr Crawford ran round and

round and Eric enjoyed himself.

'Another ride! One more, please!' said Eric.

'Eric! Bedtime!' called Jim.

'Oh, Dad! We're having a wonderful game. A few more minutes, please!' said Eric.

Jim was worried. 'Can I leave Eric with Crawford?' he thought. 'Perhaps Crawford wants to be friendly?'

'All right, Eric. But ten minutes only. Then you've got to come in,' said Jim.

Crawford looked up. 'I'll send him in, mister,' he said.

Jim went inside the hut. He still did not trust Crawford. So he listened to the conversation outside.

'You be my horse again,' said Eric.

'OK. We'll ride round once more. Then we'll play a quieter game. I'm getting tired,' said Crawford.

The second ride was as good as the first one.

'One last ride now,' said Eric.

Crawford shook his head. 'No,' he said. 'You sit down here. I've got something to tell you.'

'Is it a story?' asked Eric.

'Yes,' said Crawford. 'Do you remember the first time we met, Eric? Down by the river?'

Eric nodded.

'You found something, didn't you? And I had three guesses, didn't I?'

'Yes,' said Eric.

'I still have one more guess,' said Crawford. 'Here it is.'

'You won't guess right,' said Eric.

Crawford put his hands over his eyes. 'Yes, I can see it all now,' he said.

From inside the hut, Jim looked at Crawford and Eric.

'They're playing a guessing game,' he thought. 'I can't

stay and listen. I have some work to do. I'll call Eric in a few minutes.'

'Yes, Eric,' said Crawford. 'I can see a picture, like in a dream ... you ... and a large animal ... lying side by side.'

'You're nearly right,' said Eric. 'Nearly!'

'And she's yellow,' said Crawford. 'Yellow ... like the sun. And she's got babies with her ... One, is it? ... Or two? . . . Or three? . . .'

Eric jumped up and down.

'Yes!' he said. 'She's got two babies. But what is she?'

'I know, Eric,' said Crawford. 'She's a ... golden seal!'

'You're right! You're right!' said Eric.

'At last!' thought Crawford. 'But where have they hidden the seal?'

'Eric. Where is she?' asked Crawford.

The little boy was silent. He remembered his father's words. He must not tell Crawford about the golden seal.

'Where is the golden seal, Eric?' Crawford asked again.

'I don't know,' said Eric.

'You don't know!' said Crawford. 'But didn't you help your Dad to carry away her pelt?'

'Her pelt? But she isn't dead!' said Eric.

'Your Dad didn't shoot her?' asked Crawford.

'No,' said Eric. 'I made him promise not to. She's my friend.'

'Tell *me* where she is,' said Crawford. 'I promise I won't shoot her either.'

Eric was worried. 'Why do you want to know where she is?' he asked.

Crawford smiled. 'Golden seals are very pretty,' he said. 'But I've never seen one.'

'You want to look at her?' asked Eric.

'Yes,' said Crawford.

'OK, I'll tell you,' said Eric. 'But you must promise me never to hurt her.'

'All right,' said Crawford. 'I'll promise.'

'Say these words after me,' said Eric. ' "I promise never, never, never to hurt the golden seal. God strike me dead if I break my promise." '

Crawford repeated the little boy's words. Why not? It was only a little boy's game.

Then Eric took hold of Crawford's hand and showed him the way to the golden seal's pool.

19

Death Comes to Unimak

Eric had gone to bed and Crawford was alone. He had found a gun that Jim had hidden in the hut.

'Now the golden seal's pelt will be mine,' he thought.

Soon the lights in the hut went out. Crawford looked around him. Everything was still and very quiet. There was bright moonlight outside.

'I'll kill the seal and steal their boat,' Crawford thought. 'And I'll soon be back in Dutch Harbour.'

Silently, he got up and went out of the hut and walked to the golden seal's pool. The seal was swimming peacefully with her two pups. Crawford saw them clearly in the light of the moon. He raised his gun and pointed it between the golden seal's eyes.

Then he remembered the voice of the little boy. 'Say after me, I promise never, never, never to hurt the golden seal.'

There was a noise behind him. Crawford looked round and a bird flew away.

'I must kill the golden seal now,' Crawford thought.

Again, Crawford pointed his gun at the golden seal.

But then something moved in the shadows behind Crawford. Crawford was watching the golden seal. He heard nothing and saw nothing behind him.

Slowly, the Kodiak bear came nearer. Now it was only a few metres away.

Crawford looked round. Too late! The bear was on him. He screamed and fired his gun. The bullet hit the hard head of the Kodiak bear. But it did not kill it. Crawford saw the claws coming towards him and the huge mouth wide open.

'God strike me dead if I break my promise,' he remembered.

There was no time to shoot again. But Crawford was a hunter, he knew what to do. He took out his long knife.

But the bear attacked first. Its claws cut into Crawford's arm. The pain was terrible. But Crawford fought for his life. He moved quickly and stabbed the bear deep in the heart.

The wounded bear fell. Crawford fell too. But the bear's claws cut deep into Crawford's body and broke his bones. For Crawford, the end was near.

'God strike me dead if I break my promise,' he remembered.

Then the Kodiak bear attacked for the last time. And Crawford's body lay bleeding in the sand.

Crawford was dead and his knife was in the bear's heart. Blood poured out onto the sand.

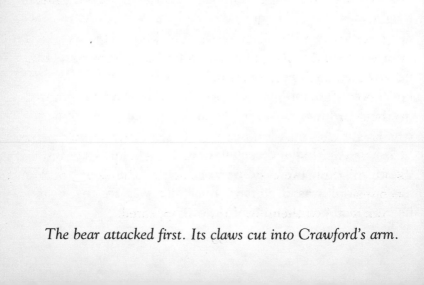

The bear attacked first. Its claws cut into Crawford's arm.

The bear's eyes looked up at the moon for the last time. And then the only living things were the golden seal and her pups in the pool.

20

At the Water's Edge

It was early morning. Crawford and the bear lay side by side on the sand. Sea-birds were flying round and round over their bodies. Jim and Tania left the children sleeping. They went to see what was happening.

'Are they both dead?' she asked.

'Yes,' said Jim. 'It's all over, Tania!'

An hour later they were burying Crawford.

After the burial, they walked back towards the hut.

'Jim,' said Tania, 'do you think Crawford killed the golden seal?'

'No,' said Jim. 'Her body wasn't there.'

'Is the golden seal still on the island, then?' asked Tania.

Jim knew what Tania was thinking. He too, had wanted to kill the golden seal. The golden seal had brought so much unhappiness.

'Look, Tania. There she is!' said Jim. And he pointed to the shore.

The golden seal and her pups were on the shore by the sea. They did not wait. They went straight into the water. Soon, all three were swimming back to the safety of the deep sea.

Jim watched them until they disappeared.

'Are you very sad?' asked Tania.

'No,' said Jim. 'I'm glad she's gone.'

Tania smiled at him and kissed him.

'I'm glad that you're glad,' she said.

Then they looked down at the river. Their river. Its water was clear in the morning light. It was beautiful, as beautiful as that other river – the river that ran out of Eden.

Points for Understanding

1

1 Why was Jim Lee's face so ugly?
2 What was Jim's job?
3 Why did most fishermen not take their boats to the island of Unimak?
4 Where were Jim and Tania married?
5 The people of Dutch Harbour said, 'Jim and the Aleut woman won't stay there very long.'
   (a)   Who was 'the Aleut woman'?
   (b)   Where was 'there'?
   (c)   Were the people of Dutch Harbour right?

2

1 Where did Jim and Tania live on Unimak?
2 What are 'pelts'?
3 Why did Jim put traps in the river?
4 Jim wanted to shoot a golden seal for two reasons. What were the two reasons?
5 How many children did Jim and Tania have? What were their names?
6 Why did Jim not enjoy his visits to Dutch Harbour?

3

1 Why are summer storms in the Aleutians so dangerous?
2 Jim saw that the sea was covered with seaweed. Why did this worry him?
3 What did Jim tell the children to do?

4

1 Why did Jim want to pull in the salmon traps from the river?
2 Why did Eric want to take his father's binoculars?
3 What promise did Eric make to his father?
4 Jim and Tania ran to their hut with their daughter, Jess. Was Eric at the hut?

5

1 When the storm began, Eric did not run home. Why?
2 Where did he shelter?
3 What did Eric find there?
4 Eric woke up in the middle of the night and he was cold. Where did he sleep?

6

1 What was Howard Hamilton Crawford doing in a ship close to Unimak?
2 Crawford saw that the storm was very near. Why did he not go back to his ship?
3 Crawford saw a light. Where was the light? What did Crawford do?

7

1 Why did Jim decide to look for Eric?
2 Why did Jim tie a rope round his waist?
3 Did Jim find anything when he went out in the storm?
4 What did Tania do for Jim when he was back in the hut?
5 What did Tania ask Jim to promise her?
6 'Don't let him in!' screamed Tania.
   (a)   Who did Tania say was at the door?
   (b)   Who came into their hut?

8

1 Why could Jim not open the man's anorak?
2 Each time Tania looked at the man, his eyes were shut. But what did Tania think?
3 'We're staying awake because of our son,' Jim told the stranger.
   (a) Who was the stranger?
   (b) Did he believe Jim?
4 The stranger wanted to go with Jim and his family to look for Eric. Why?
5 Did Jim like the stranger? What did the stranger put into his pocket?

9

1 Eric told the seal about his father. He wanted his father to make a promise. What was the promise?
2 Why was it going to be very difficult to cross the river?
3 Why was Crawford happy when he saw Eric?
4 Why did Crawford not want to walk ten kilometres up the river?
5 Why could Jim not swim across the river?
6 Tania looked at Crawford. Crawford understood what she wanted to say.
   What did she want to say?

10

1 Jim looked at Tania. Suddenly he became jealous. Why?
2 Eric said Crawford could have three guesses.
   (a) What were Crawford's first two guesses?
   (b) Why did Crawford not make a third guess?
3 Crawford carried Eric safely across the river. Then he told himself that he was a fool. Why?
4 Why did Tania jump away from Crawford?

11

1 Eric asked his father to make a promise. What other promise did Jim remember?
2 After he made the promise to his son, Jim was angry with himself. Why?

12

1 'I think I'll go for a walk,' said Crawford. What did Jim think Crawford wanted to do?
2 What did Jim ask Tania to do?
3 Tania asked, 'Jim, what is happening?' Why could Jim not give her the true answer?
4 What did Jim find on the floor of the storm hut?
5 Where was the golden seal?
6 Why could Jim not shoot the golden seal?

13

1 'Yes. A secret between you and me and Mummy,' said Jim.
   (a)   Why was Eric surprised when Jim said this?
   (b)   What else did Jim tell him?
2 Why did Jim not try to shoot the Kodiak bear?
3 Suddenly Jim began to run home. Why?

14

1 Crawford remembered a story he had heard in Dutch Harbour. What was the story?
2 Why did Tania fire the gun at Crawford? Did she hit him?
3 What did Tania decide to tell Jim about the noise of the gun?
4 Why did Jim believe her immediately?

15

1 When he woke up, Jim heard a noise.
   (a)   Who had made the noise?
   (b)   What was happening?
2 'Perhaps it's true,' thought Jim. What was Jim thinking about?
3 The voice of the devil spoke to Jim.
   What was the voice saying?
4 What was Jim's reply to the voice?

16

1 When Tania woke up, she saw that Jim and Crawford had gone
   outside. What was she afraid of?
2 Tania remembered her wedding promise.
   (a)   What had she promised?
   (b)   What did she decide to do?
3 Jim and Tania put all the pelts into their boat. What was Jim going
   to do?
4 Howard Crawford was a very angry man. Why?

17

1 What did Crawford believe Jim had done?
2 How did Crawford make Jim very angry?
3 After Jim took Crawford's gun, Crawford was left alone in the hut.
   What question did Crawford ask himself? What did he decide to do
   next time?

1 Why did Eric not want to go to bed?
2 What was the first game Crawford played with Eric?
3 'Then we'll play a quieter game,' Crawford said to Eric.
   (a)   What was the quieter game?
   (b)   Why did Crawford want to play this game?
4 Did Crawford know if the golden seal was alive or dead?
5 Crawford made a promise to Eric. What were the words of this promise?
6 Did Crawford believe that promises were important?

19

1 The first time Crawford pointed his gun at the golden seal, he heard a voice in his head.
   (a)   Whose voice did he hear?
   (b)   What was the voice saying?
2 The second time Crawford pointed his gun at the seal, something moved behind him. What was it?
3 What did Crawford remember before he died?
4 Which animal had Crawford killed?

1 'Are you very sad?' Tania asked Jim.
   (a)   What had they seen?
   (b)   What was Jim's reply to Tania's question?
   (c)   Was Tania pleased with Jim's reply?

The Lost World by Sir Arthur Conan Doyle
A Christmas Carol by Charles Dickens
Riders of the Purple Sage by Zane Grey
The Canterville Ghost and Other Stories by Oscar Wilde
Lady Portia's Revenge and Other Stories by David Evans
The Picture of Dorian Gray by Oscar Wilde
Treasure Island by Robert Louis Stevenson
Road to Nowhere by John Milne
The Black Cat by John Milne
Don't Tell Me What To Do by Michael Hardcastle
The Runaways by Victor Canning
The Red Pony by John Steinbeck
The Goalkeeper's Revenge and Other Stories by Bill Naughton
The Stranger by Norman Whitney
The Promise by R. L. Scott-Buccleuch
The Man With No Name by Evelyn Davies and Peter Town
The Cleverest Person in the World by Norman Whitney
Claws by John Landon
Z for Zachariah by Robert C. O'Brien
Tales of Horror by Bram Stoker
Frankenstein by Mary Shelley
Silver Blaze and Other Stories by Sir Arthur Conan Doyle
Tales of Ten Worlds by Arthur C. Clarke
The Boy Who Was Afraid by Armstrong Sperry
Room 13 and Other Ghost Stories by M. R. James
The Narrow Path by Francis Selormey
The Woman in Black by Susan Hill

For further information on the full selection of
Readers at all five levels in the series, please refer
to the Heinemann ELT Guided Readers catalogue.

Macmillan Heinemann English Language Teaching

Between Towns Road, Oxford OX4 3PP, UK

A division of Macmillan Publishers Limited

Companies and representatives throughout the world

ISBN 0 435 27319 1

Heinemann is a registered trade mark of Reed Educational & Professional Publishing Ltd

A River Ran Out of Eden first published in United Kingdom by
Hodder and Stoughton Ltd, 1962
© Donald Payne 1962
This retold version by Peter Hodson for Heinemann ELT Guided Readers
First published 1978
Reprinted 1982, 1984, 1985, 1987

Illustrated by Michael Charlton
Typography by Adrian Hodgkins
Designed by Sue Vaudin
Cover by Tracey O'Dea and Marketplace Design
Typeset in 11.5/14.5 pt Goudy
Printed and bound in Spain by Mateu Cromo S.A.

2004 2003 2002 2001 2000
13 12 11 10 9 8 7 6 5 4